# A NUMBER OF
# ANIMALS

# A NUMBER OF ANIMALS

# CHRISTOPHER WORMELL

CREATIVE EDITIONS

A Number of Animals
written by Kate Green,
illustrated by Christopher Wormell

Text copyright © 1993 by Kate Green
Illustrations copyright © 1993 by Christopher Wormell
Designed by Ian Butterworth

Published in 1993 by Creative Editions
123 South Broad Street, Mankato, Minnesota 56001 USA

Creative Editions is an imprint of Creative Education, Inc.

The publication of this book is a joint venture between
Creative Education, Inc. and American Education Publishing.

Library of Congress Cataloging-in-Publication Data

Wormell, Christopher
A number of animals / illustrations and story idea by
Christopher Wormell : text by Kate Green

Summary: Introduces the numbers one through ten as
a little lost chick searches everywhere for his mother.

ISBN 1-56846-083-X

1. Counting--Juvenile literature.
2. Domestic animals--Juvenile literature.
[1. Counting.  2. Domestic animals.]
I. Green, Kate. II. Title.
QA113.W67 1993
513.2'11--dc20
[E]                      93-17134
Printed in Italy.

For Daisy

# I
## Chick

One little chick, lost and alone.

# 2
## Horses

Two huge horses back by the stable.
"Have you seen my mother?"
"Not today," the horses neigh.

# 3
## Cows

Three slow cows sunning in the meadow.
"Have *you* seen my mother?"
But all they do is moo.

# 4

## Turkeys

Four fat turkeys ruffling their feathers.
"Gobble, gobble!" they gab
and strut through the straw.

# 5
## Goats

Five shaggy goats grazing in the field.
Their beards are hairy. Their horns are sharp.
"Baa-aa," they bleat. "No hens here!"

# 6
## Geese

Six white geese waddling toward the water.

The little chick comes too close.

*Look out!*

# Sheep

Seven sleepy sheep, woolly and warm.
The world is too big when you're all alone.

# 8
## Ducks

Eight splashing ducks calling quack, quack, quack.
The chick cheeps to them,
but the ducks don't quack back.

## Pigs

Nine pudgy pigs flopped in the mud.
"Wake up!" peeps the chick–
but what does he hear?

# 10
## Chicks

It's his sisters chirping and his brothers cheeping!
Now there are ten chicks...

…and one mother hen!
"Here you are!" the little chick squeaks
and all ten follow her home.

1

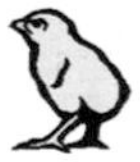

2

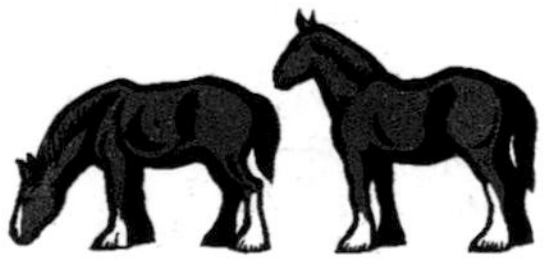

3

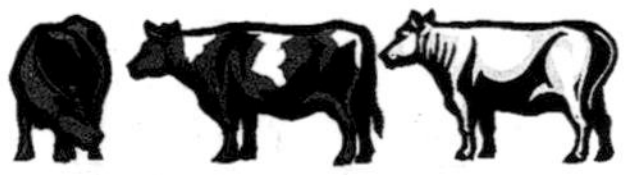

4

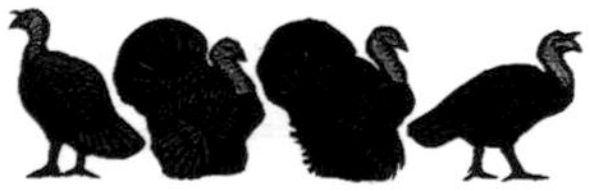

5

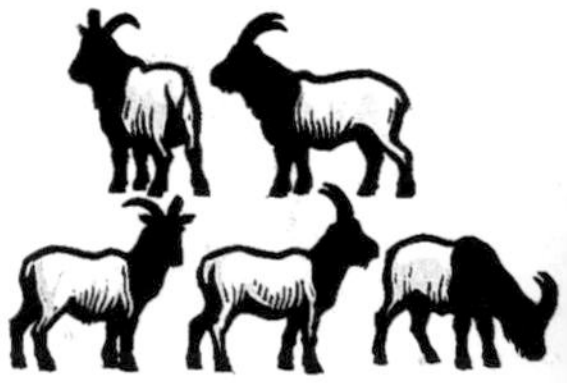

6 7 8 9 10